Carrie Lynn and the Science Project

by

Rob Gray

PublishAmerica
Baltimore

First printing

ISBN: 1-4137-1754-3
PUBLISHED BY PUBLISHAMERICA, LLLP
www.publishamerica.com
Baltimore

Printed in the United States of America

Some historians believe that over 10,000 years ago, in what is now the Atlantic Ocean, there was an island continent inhabited by a race of people that were far more advanced than even modern man is today. They had palaces made of marble and temples to their gods fashioned of gold and silver.

Due to artifacts found in certain locations, it is theorized that these people had harnessed the power of electricity and other forms of energy and that they had mental and physical capabilities that could only be described as super human. It is unknown exactly how these ancient people were able to accomplish these feats. Some say they may have been aliens from another planet, others believe they were simply another race of people that evolved independently from the rest of the world. Still others say that they learned how to use their brains to their fullest capacity. While modern man, it is believed, uses only a fruction of his mental capability, the inhabitants of this island used all of theirs.

Most of what we know about these people was gathered from scholars' writings over the past ten millennia with a good portion coming from books gathered in the ancient library of Alexandria. Unfortunately, the tragic loss of the great library by Marc Anthony's fire caused most of its knowledge of the ancient world to be lost forever.

One book on the subject survived the fire and from it we learn that the people there were believed to have had a vast knowledge of plants and minerals and were able to concoct medicines of great healing power.

According to this source one of the reasons for their extraordinary power might have been something in their diet...

Carrie Lynn's eyelids started to droop and she had to force them up in order to focus on the words, but the urge to sleep was too strong and she drifted off. She was just starting to get serious about this nap when...

"Carrie Lynn, come on honey, you're going to be late for practice."

The voice coming from downstairs was Carrie Lynn's mother.

"Ok Mom," she said groggily as the smoke cleared and she remembered where she was. She put her hair ribbon on the page, closed the book she was reading and tossed it on the bed as she went down stairs.

INTRODUCTION

Our universe is a huge, wonderful and mysterious place. From the largest planet to the smallest bit of matter, scientists have been trying to learn about it, understand and decipher it since man first discovered-fire, planted a seed, or noticed the stars gliding across the sky. Though, it seems every time we figure something out, we realize just how little we really know. Take one little hydrogen atom and two tiny oxygen atoms, put them together, and presto you have water! That's nothing for nature to do but not quite as easy for mere man to accomplish. You might think, one atom, or molecule more or less couldn't make that much difference...but, add one or take one away, and it could make all the difference in the world.

Carrie Lynn Foster, a bright and pretty fifth grader at Mayobrook Elementary School, is about to do a science project — just another ordinary science project with a display board, test tubes, hypothesis and results? Well, not exactly. Carrie Lynn will soon discover something that no one has ever seen before or will ever see again, at least in our lifetime. For this little girl is about to reveal a secret of nature that takes just the right combination to unlock...something that will turn her world completely around, and she won't even know how she does it. It's just another one of those little mysteries of the universe.

ONE

The girl ran over to the bench, out of breath and sweaty, and handed her mouth guard, goalie gloves and shin guards to her mother. Eager to find her drink, she routed through the Nike gym bag. "Mom, where's my Gatorade?" she asked, but before her mother could answer she continued, "Can I spend the night at Kim's...please?"

Her mother was gathering up the necessities of soccer practice and putting them unto the equipment bag when she turned and said, "I told you not to ask me about spending the night with anyone 'till we get this science project done. It's due Monday and you have your reading to do, and you still have to do your experiments."

"But Mom!" Carrie Lynn Foster said, tucking her blond hair behind her ears. She pushed her bottom lip out and tried to blow her bangs out of her face but they were stuck to her forehead with perspiration.

"No buts!" her mother said as they started walking toward the car. "If we get it done this weekend then maybe you can stay over next weekend."

"We still have to do ours too, honey," Jenny Bayer, Kim's mom, told Carrie Lynn.

The girls ran over to some of the other team members and

were talking and giggling as girls do.

"By the way, what is Kim's project about this time?" Katherine asked.

"Well, all I can say right now is I've got a lot of mold growing in my refrigerator," said Jenny, "and this time they're not growing on my leftovers."

Katherine laughed and said, "Ooh, sounds interesting."

"How about Carrie?"

"She won't tell us. It has something to do with sugar and baking soda and her Easy Bake Oven," Katherine said. "She asked me to buy the ingredients I didn't already have, but she won't let on what it's all about. We'll write it all out when she finishes her experiment…whatever it is."

"I can't wait to see it," said Jenny.

"Well, see you at practice," said Katherine. "Bye Kimmie."

"Good-bye, Miss Katherine. See ya at school Carrie," Kim said.

"Good-bye."

"Good-bye."

It was just about 7:00 pm when Michael Foster pulled into the driveway of his home. Another late day at the office, and boy was he up for a nice dinner and some Friday night relaxation. Katherine must have been hard at work in the yard all day because the grass was cut and the trimming was done; everything looked great.

She sure does take good care of this place, he thought. He noticed his wife's car was not there which meant that they weren't home from lacrosse practice, or was it soccer this time? Oh well, just the same, he was hungry and was hoping something was simmering on the stove. As he unlocked the back door and walked in, the youngest member of the family, Hazel their cat, greeted him. With her black fur and hazel-green eyes she was the perfect witch's companion.

"Hi, Haze," he said, but she didn't respond, she just shimmied her way around him and out the door to the porch. "Yes, I did have a good day, thanks."

Hazel is an indoor cat, but she loves sit on the back porch and think she's outside. She can see all the wildlife out in the yard, but she can't get at it. She's happy enough watching it. Although she will, on occasion, slip out to see it close up and the whole family has to go out and search for her. But, they always find her close to by, she knows her home.

"And how was your day?" he asked as he watched her leave for the evening show, not really expecting an answer.

He tried to detect a sumptuous aroma in the air, pot roast maybe or meat loaf perhaps. Nothing was immediately noticeable, but he didn't give up hope. He entered the kitchen and looked into the oven, maybe chicken potpie…nothing.

"Oh well, I guess I better whip up something."

He cut up some celery and onions, garlic and carrots, opened a jar of store-bought spaghetti sauce and put on some noodles to cook.

"Good thing I'm a great cook! Take some store-bought sauce and add a few things to it and viola, dinner!"

As the sauce was beginning to take on that tempting fragrance, the door opened and Carrie Lynn ran in to greet her father. "Hi Dad!" she said as she ran over and gave him one of her big bear hugs. "Me strong like bull!" she said.

"Oh, you sure are."

"What's cooking?" she asked.

"Just some spaghetti I whipped up. Are you hungry?" her dad asked.

"Sure, but not too much sauce please," Carrie Lynn said as she ran off in the direction of her room.

"I like that," he said almost to himself. "You slave over a hot stove all day creating a masterpiece and she doesn't want too much sauce! Humph. You can help me set the table when you get back," he called after her.

"Hi honey," Mom said as she came in the kitchen lugging in Carrie Lynn's soccer equipment. "Sorry about dinner, it just got late and I was lost in my yard work."

"How was practice? Was it soccer or lacrosse?"

"Michael, Tuesdays it's lacrosse and Fridays it's soccer."

"Ok. By the way, where is Matthew?"

"He asked if he could go over to Alex's after school to practice lacrosse a while. I told him to be home by dinner time. By the way, have you seen Carrie Lynn's Friday folder this week?" Mom asked.

"No, I just got here and started fixing dinner. I haven't seen anything."

"Well, she did well in spelling and comprehension but she got a C on a geography test and a D on a math paper."

Just then they heard a scream coming from upstairs, Carrie Lynn came running into the kitchen. "Mom, Mom, Matthew took my last Snickers bar! I told him to stay out of my room, the brat."

"Michael, you are going to have to talk with that boy

again."

"OK, I guess our last little chat didn't take."

"I guess not! If I catch him in my room again, I'm going to really get even," said the distraught little girl.

"Now Carrie Lynn, don't blow this up into a big fight. I'll talk to him again and he'll stay out of your room. I promise," said her dad. "Now will you please help me set the table for dinner?"

"Ok," Carrie Lynn grumbled.

Michael handed her the knives, forks and napkins. He carried the plates and glasses to the table.

"You two want salads?" Dad asked everyone.

"I do," said Mom.

"I'll take a small one," said Carrie Lynn. "With Ranch."

Dad went back for the salad bowls.

Just then Matthew Foster made his entrance. Matthew is Carrie Lynn's older brother by three years. He's an eighth grader at Central Middle School and generally a pretty good kid. Already almost as tall as his dad, he has his sandy blond hair and his passion for playing the guitar. He loves sports, has always been a good student and, except for his enjoyment of tormenting his younger sister now and then, gets along with just about everybody. Following Matthew into the kitchen is Alex Williams, Matthew's best friend. Alex is not as tall as Matthew and not as heavy but he has a lot of talent for sports so the two of them practice together all the time. With freckles and spectacles that always seem to be sliding down his nose (the glasses, not the freckles) and his red hair, Alex always reminded Michael of Woody Allen. Both boys were carrying lacrosse sticks and gloves and wearing cleats.

"Out!" Mom shouted. "Matthew, how many times have I told you not to wear your cleats *in-to-thee* house. You bring dirt in all over my floors and put holes in my rugs…hi, Alex how are you?"

"Fine, Mrs. Foster how are you? Sorry about the cleats, you forget you're wearing them sometimes. My mom gets upset too if I wear 'em into the house," said Alex.

"I bet she does. You boys don't realize how much work it is to take care of a house and keep it clean and then have one of you kids track it all up with dusty shoes."

"Alex…" Michael started to say.

"Hi, Mr. Foster."

"…Have you eaten?"

"No sir."

"Want some spaghetti?"

"Sure!" said Alex, pushing up his glasses.

"Carrie Lynn, would you get another plate please?" said dad.

"We don't need another plate Dad," Carrie Lynn said sweetly.

"We don't?"

"No, Alex can have Matthew's plate, THE JERK!"

"What!" Matthew speaks for the first time.

"Now Carrie Lynn…" said Dad.

"What's her problem?" said a slightly shocked Matthew.

"I'll tell you my problem, nimrod. You broke into my room and stole my last Snickers bar!"

"Uh, well…you've had it since Easter."

"I was saving it."

"For what, Christmas?"

"It's none of your business how long she's had it, Matthew," said Mom.

"Matthew, for the last time, stay out of you sister's room!" Dad said.

"Ok, ok, I'll get her another stupid Snickers bar," said Matthew, and then to Carrie Lynn, "with my own money."

"Ok?" said Dad to Carrie Lynn.

"Ok."

"Well then, let's eat," said Dad. "I'm hungry, come and get it."

TWO

The next day, everyone slept a little late but Dad was up first by habit. He put on his slippers and went to the porch to get the newspaper. One of the things he really enjoyed was reading the paper on Saturday mornings alone when everyone else was still asleep. Sometimes when the weather is nice he'll sit on the porch with his paper, cup of coffee, read and just watch the day begin.

Forty minutes or so went by and he hadn't heard any stirring from inside the house so he went in to investigate. Matthew was up watching TV in the family room, and Carrie Lynn was still asleep (she did like her rest). He didn't see Mom anywhere until he glanced out of their bedroom window. There she was, over by the shed, putting a bag of something into the wheel barrow.

"Oh well, I guess I better start breakfast," he said.

Dad made bacon, scrambled eggs with cheese, fried potatoes and toast. By the time everything was ready everyone was finally awake.

"Come and get it," he announced to the whole house.

Carrie Lynn came in. "No thanks, Dad. I don't want to eat anything before my game."

"What?" he said.

"Just wheat toast for me, honey," said Mom.

"How about you, son?" asked Dad. "Are you having anything?"

"Sure, fill 'er up," Matthew said, picking up a plate.

"Well, at least it's not all going to waste," said Dad a little disappointedly.

After breakfast Katherine caught Matthew by himself and took the opportunity to discuss something with him.

"Honey," she started. "Would you do your father and me a favor?"

"Sure."

"Carrie Lynn brought home some pretty bad papers in her Friday folder yesterday and you are so good at math, we were hoping you would tutor her again, like you did last time."

"What? Mom!"

"We would help her, but you can communicate with her more on her level. You know the latest ways they teach things. The last time your dad tried to show her his way of doing things it just confused her and it didn't help."

"Mom, sometimes when I just talk to her she acts so goofy that what I say just doesn't seem to get through. And you want me to help her with math? I swear sometimes..." he interrupted himself, "you know how they say we only use about ten percent of our brain, I'd say that she only uses about half of her ten percent."

"Now, you stop that! You sister is a very bright, intelligent girl. She has a nice personality and a quick mind. She just has a little trouble with math, as a lot of kids do. She'll get it if you give her a little help. She's growing and kids go through difficult stages. You certainly have your moments," Mom scolded Matthew. And then she softened, "Please."

"Ok Mom, but if she starts acting goofy it's all over."

"She won't, I promise," said Mom.

Later, as they were getting ready to go to Carrie Lynn's soccer game, Mom explained to her what they were going to do later. "Carrie Lynn, after the game, you know what you're doing?" she asked.

"Yes Mom…science project," said Carrie Lynn reluctantly.

"Right, you're going to do your experiment, write down your results and then you're going to go over a few of your school papers. I see you are having a few problems here and there," her mom said.

"Oh Mom!" said the girl with a very nice whine in her voice.

"And, we're going to get some help from non other than your favorite Snicker stealing brother."

"Noooooooooo, not Brat-hew I mean Matthew!" was all that Carrie Lynn was able to get out as her throat constricted in protest.

"Oh yes. The last time he helped you, you did improve, and Matthew has graciously consented to do to again."

"Maybe he did, but I'm not!"

"Oh yes you will, or no spending the night with anyone for a month."

"Mom!"

"Carrie Lynn, I'm not kidding," said Mom adamantly.

"Ok, ok. I'll do it…but I won't like it."

"There's my favorite little girl. See, threats work every time, and when you're finished with your studying we'll start putting the science project together. Now give us a smile."

"How can I smile, when my whole weekend is taken up by school work?" she said frowning.

"Just think honey, when this is all over, you can have all next weekend to do any thing you want."

All Carrie Lynn Foster was able to accomplish at this was a closed mouth prissy little grin that said, "Ok, you win this time."

After the game, which the girls won three to two, and after a fruitless plea that she be allowed to go over Kim's house instead of going home, Carrie Lynn rode back with her family to start the project.

"Pretty good game there, squirt," Matthew said as they got in the car. "You and Chloe and Kim are about the best players on the team."

"Thanks," was all that Carrie Lynn could muster up in response. She was thinking about the tortuous time that she would have with him later as he tried to explain fractions!

When they arrived at home Matthew went up to his room to do some reading and play his guitar, and Dad set about repairing some screen on the back porch. Carrie Lynn followed Mom to the kitchen.

"Now let's get your stuff together for the experiment. You wanted flour, water, baking powder, baking soda, yeast, sugar and your Easy Bake Oven, right?" asked Mom. "Sounds to me like you are going to bake cookies, not do a science project."

"Mom, it has to do with cake and how it rises, or not, depending on what you mix in the ingredients. I'm going to try to bake a cake without baking powder and make it rise anyway," she said.

"Ok, what do you need me to do?"

"Nothing, I'll be alright, but if I need help can I call you?"

"Sure you can. Ok, if you need me I'll be outside spreading some mulch around my peonies."

"Ok, Mom."

Just then Dad, who was still working on the porch, poked his head in the back door and said to Katherine, "What's for lunch, hon?"

"Nothing yet. Carrie Lynn's doing her experiment right now. We'll have to eat later."

"Aw!" Dad said returning to his work.

Mom and Carrie Lynn looked at each other and laughed.

"Dad sure does like to eat, doesn't he?"

"He sure does, I'm surprised he's not as big as a house," said Katherine shaking her head.

Dad opened the door again and said, "I heard that."

"Oops," Mom said.

"By the way, girls," Michael said as he tossed Hazel in, "don't let her out on the porch 'till I'm finished with the screen. She may get out, ok?"

"Ok, Dad I'll keep her in here with me while I do my experiment." She set her down on the stool next to the table, "now you sit there and watch and be a good girl," Carrie Lynn said to Hazel. "I'll let you out later."

Mom left and Carrie Lynn began her experiment. For the

next hour and a half she mixed and measured and baked, and baked and measured and mixed. She put together as accurately as she could all of the ingredients and varied the necessary amounts just right. After a while, she had seven cakes done, some rose pretty high and some just lay there like pancakes. Her results were pretty promising and her hypothesis was correct. Without just the right amount of baking powder, which produces just the right amount of carbon dioxide, you either get too much rise in your cakes or not enough. She kept pretty meticulous notes on her experiments but wanted her mom or dad to help her organize it and make a graph.

Boy, she thought, *I'm doing pretty good, Mom will be impressed. Maybe she won't make me go over my papers with "Brathew".*

She thought she had enough ingredients for one more cake and, so, to make an even eight, she started to mix everything. Four tablespoons of plain flour, a pinch of salt, one tablespoon of margarine, two tablespoons of sugar, two tablespoons of milk and, this time just ¼ teaspoon of baking powder.

Just then, Matthew came into the kitchen looking for something to eat.

"How's it going, squirt? Boy, this stuff smells pretty good. Mind if I just have a taste?" he said, as he reached for one of Carrie Lynn's cakes.

"Mommmmmmmm!!!" Carrie Lynn yelled. "Get away, those are for my science project, Mommmmm!"

Immediately Matthew backed away. Hazel, who had been watching all this time, looked a little frightened from all the noise.

"Ok ok, I was only kidding," he said raising his hands up like a crook that was just captured by the police. He tried to calm his sister so she wouldn't call their mom. "Look, I just want to get something to drink and I'm outta here."

Hazel yawned and watched as Matthew got a glass down from the cupboard and took the root beer out of the refrigerator. He set the glass down next to the bowl in which Carrie Lynn was mixing her last cake. She went back to her recipe, keeping her eye on him the whole time. As he poured the root beer into the glass, Matthew noticed that two drops splashed into the bowl as she was stirring.

"Eeek!" He thought as he looked up at her quickly to see if she noticed — she hadn't. He put the plastic bottle back in the refrigerator. "Whew!"

"Well, have fun, I'll see you later," he said as he picked up his drink and started back to his room.

"Humph," was about all she could say as she kept her eye on him leaving.

As she watched until he disappeared around the corner, she couldn't see the chemical-reaction taking place in the bowl. She didn't notice the little electric spark in the cake batter as it flashed in the middle, spiraled out to the edges, and then disappeared. She did notice the puff of smoke as it drifted up and out of the bowl. She waved it away with her hand and looked closely at the batter to see if it was ok.

"Now, that's strange," she said in amazement.

What just happened was something that hasn't happened in the last 10,000 years and probably won't again for another 10,000. With that *exact* amount of molecules, ones that make up such everyday substances as milk, margarine, sugar, salt, flour, and baking powder, those two drops of root beer reacted to create a substance rarely seen in our world. The tumblers fell in just the right combination to unlock one of the secrets of the universe. There was no big explosion, no bolt of lightning, but when Carrie Lynn Foster pours the mixture into the cake pan and slides it into her Easy Bake oven to cook, something's going to happen that will completely disrupt the little girl's life if not forever…at least for the next few days.

THREE

Carrie Lynn took that last cake out of the oven and after it cooled, tried to lift it out of the pan, but as cakes go this one wasn't very good. It just crumbled and fell apart.

"Oh!" Carrie Lynn said with disgust. "I can't use this one, it's all crumbs. What happened?"

She was almost in tears when her dad popped his head in the door. He was about to ask if lunch was ready when he saw that she was upset at something and came in to see if he could help.

"What's the matter, honey?" he asked.

"Oh, look at this stupid cake. It was the last of my batter too, and I can't make another one."

"Well, what about the rest of these? They look pretty good."

"I know, but I was hoping to make an even eight cakes, 'til the last one disintegrated," she said, putting her arms around his waist and giving him a hug, but what she really wanted was one from him.

He gave her one back and said, "Oh, you're strong like bull!"

She gave him a half-hearted smile.

"Aw, forget that one, you've done a good job here and I

can tell you've got good results. Let me see, it has something to do with what it takes to make a cake rise, right?" he asked.

"Well yeah, something like that."

"See, it's obvious, from what you already have that you've got a very good science project here," he consoled her. "Come on, I'll help you clean up and we can organize your data while it's still fresh in your mind."

Carrie Lynn gathered her note papers together while Dad started filling the sink with soapy water. She collected all the dirty cake pans and bowls and brought them to the sink. She picked up the plate that had the crummy cake in it, brought it over to the trash can and was about to toss it in when she thought, *Well, it won't be a total loss I'll just eat this one.* She scooped it into a zip-lock baggie and took it to her room to hide it from "Bratboy".

On the top shelf in her closet was an old hat box she had labeled "Barbie clothes", she took it down. There weren't any Barbie clothes in it, but all of the belongings she wanted to keep private. Among other things, there was a tin can which held her rock collection, a cloth bag with some old coins her grandfather had given her and a black glass frog her father had gotten for her from a flea market. She put the crummy cake in there and then went back to help her dad with the dishes.

After lunch, where Dad made everyone grilled cheese sandwiches with American and Swiss cheese with ham and tomato and a cup of vegetable soup, Carrie Lynn and her mom and dad went down the basement to set about compiling the experiment data and constructing the display board. They decided to put the project together before they went over Carrie Lynn's school papers, which was ok with her.

The longer they put that off the better, Carrie Lynn thought.

Hazel, the kitty, joined them and helped by laying all over their art board, charts and diagrams, and leaving black cat fur on everything.

"Get outta here, you," Mom said as she shooed her off of their project, but Hazel just scooted over a foot or two and plopped down on the next batch of papers. "Oh, you're a lot of help!"

When they were finished, they admired their work.

"Carrie Lynn, I'm very proud of you. You did an excellent job on your experiment," said her mother.

"You really did, honey," added her father.

"And for all of your hard work, missy," her mom continued as she handed her a big bag of Snickers bars, "a special reward."

"Wow, thanks Mom!"

"Well, you deserve it, and make sure you hide them so *you know who* doesn't get a hold of them," said her father.

"Oh, I will."

Carrie Lynn took Hazel and the bag of Snickers to her room. She thought she might have just one before dinner and so she opened the bag, took one and put the empty wrapper on the nightstand. She was tired from all of her hard work and thought she might turn in early. She closed the door, opened the closet door and took down the hat box. As she made room for the bag of candy, she noticed the crumbled cake in there and decided to try some. After all, she had made eight cakes and didn't even taste one! She opened the bag and scooped about a third of the crumbs into her hand and popped them into her mouth.

Hum, not bad, she thought. *It's a little dry, but sweet and tastes something like...*

Whoa! All of a sudden there was a flash of light, like someone had taken her picture with a flash camera, only brighter, and her vision went blurry for a moment. The first thing she noticed was she felt dizzy. The room was spinning around and then it sounded like someone had just turned the sound track of the whole world way up. There was a rush of noise coming from everywhere. She covered her ears but that didn't seem to help very much. Hazel jumped down from the bed and, instead of her usual silent landing, she sounded like someone dropping a bag of potatoes on the floor.

The noise went on for a few minutes and Carrie Lynn was starting to get scared. She almost called her mom, but then it began to subside. As she was getting used to the sounds she found that they weren't really extra loud, but that she was hearing things from farther away than before, and all jumbled together. She found that if she closed her eyes for a moment and concentrated, she could filter out the background noises and kind of zero in on a subject. For instance, somewhere out there she could hear her mother's voice and by trying real hard she could tune her in as if her mom were on the radio. She could hear her mom and dad talking in the basement, way down stairs, just like they were in the next room.

"...You know Kathy," she could hear her father saying, "I

think Carrie Lynn wanted to do this whole project by herself to try to make up for the bad science paper she got last week."

"Well I don't know, but I sure am proud of the way she did the experimenting all by herself, and the way she cleaned up afterwards," she said.

Carrie Lynn thought, *This is really weird, I can hear them just like they were outside my door*. She opened her door and looked out into the hall just to make sure they weren't out there, it was empty. She listened on.

"She really is a good little girl," her father said.

Carrie Lynn smiled at that.

"I just hope Matthew can help her with her math problems," said her mom.

Carrie Lynn *didn't* smile at that, in fact she dreaded the thought. Then she heard her dad say, "I'm sure he can. Well, what's for supper Snookie? I'm awful hungry."

"I'm sorry, Michael, I've got to finish putting in my Princess Spirea. It's supposed to rain tomorrow and I've got five more to put in," she heard her mom say.

"Ok, if you want I can whip up some of my world famous French onion soup and a salad," he said.

"That sounds wonderful, honey," said Katherine as she started up the stairs.

"Hum, I wonder how Princess Spirea tastes?" her dad said to himself.

Carrie Lynn smiled again. "Oh Dad!" she said out loud, feeling funny that she was alone in the room.

Hum, I wonder if I can tune in on Brathew, she said to herself as she started concentrating in his direction. She found him on the phone talking to Alex.

"…Virginia said so," she could hear Matthew saying. "Yeah, she told Laurie that if you were to ask her, she'd like to go out or something."

Then, as if Alex were there in the room too she heard him say, "She did not!"

"She did, I'm not kidding."

"Wow! She's cute too," Alex said.

"Wow, she's cute too," Carrie Lynn mocked her brother's friend and laughed.

Boy, I don't know what's going on, but this is cool, she thought. *Who else can I listen to?*

She tried to zero in on her friend Kim Bayer to see if she could hear her, but she didn't know where to direct her thoughts. All she heard was a lot of people all talking at the same time, just like at the play ground at recess. Then she found that if she concentrated she could make the sounds stop, and if she listened real hard she could start them again. *Kim must be too far away to be heard*, Carrie Lynn thought. There must be a limit as to how far away she could hear people.

"Let's check on Matthew again," she said to herself. He was still on the phone.

"…Well, if coach puts Davie in as goalie again, I don't think we have much of a chance against Allentown," Alex was saying.

"I don't know, " Matthew said. "He's not that bad, he's better than their goalie."

Bor-ing, Carrie Lynn thought, *I liked it better when they were talking about girls.*

FOUR

Hazel jumped up on the bed and curled up with Carrie Lynn as she lay down for a while to rest. She had turned off the sound machine in her head and it was nice and quiet in the house. As she started to drift off to sleep, a dream was forming way in the back of her mind. It was unlike any dream she ever had before. As it brought itself into her slumbering consciousness she started to see things never seen before, even in her dreams. Colors and lights like she'd never before imagined. She even seemed to be thinking in a totally new way. It was strange and weird, but not at all frightening. No, in fact it was like a dream created in Disneyland, and just as she started to really get into it…

Knock, knock, knock. She heard banging echo in the background, but didn't know where it was coming from. Bang, bang, bang!

"Come on squirt, are you in there?" came her brother's voice.

Why was he messing up her wonderful dream? She was gliding through a sea of blue and silver sparkles when she realized it was Matthew pounding at her door. She reluctantly swam to the surface, opened her eyes, and rolled out if bed. She went to the door, opened it and just stood there as if to say, "What do you want?"

"Surprise. It's time to go over our papers," Matthew said with a smile.

"Go away!"

"Nope, Mom asked me to help you, and I said I would, so here I am," he said. As he stepped into her room, forcing Carrie Lynn to step aside, he noticed the candy wrapper on the nightstand.

"Mom said I did such a good job on my project that you don't have to help me now," Carrie Lynn said, with her fingers crossed behind her back.

"She did not, I just talked to her," he said. "So let's go I ain't got all night."

"Ain't is slang, and inappropriate language, that persons of good breeding and advanced vocabulary don't use…and you are tutoring me?" Carrie Lynn said, wondering where *that* thought came from, as she handed him her Friday folder.

"Whoa! Some pretty big words, for such a little mind there, shrimp," said her brother. "Now can we get this over with? Let's see, you are having problems with fractions, right? Proper and improper fractions, you should know all this by now." Matthew reads form the test paper; "Write each improper fraction as a mixed or whole number, twenty-nine fourths. Now, how would you do that?"

"I don't know," Carrie Lynn said in a *la de dah* kind of voice.

"Ok, you know how to divide, right? All you have to do is divide the denominator into the numerator and put the remainder over the denominator."

"The denominator and the remainder and the stupid numerator, I get confused at all that," she said.

"Look, don't let the terms confuse you, just divide the bottom number into the top number and put what's left over, over the bottom number," Matthew said.

"Let's see, four into twenty-nine is…" Carrie Lynn began, (totally unsure of herself as she started to count on her fingers), "six, with five left over."

"Six?" Matthew just stared at her. "You know, I really do believe you only use half of your brain. Ok, let's try this one. Which is larger, three fourths or five sixths?"

Carrie Lynn was starting to get frustrated, she was really trying, but she just didn't get it. She was almost in tears when she started to really concentrate on the numbers. Somewhere in the background she heard Matthew saying, "Six times four is twenty-four…"

Just then a light went on in her head, a bright light. She closed her eyes for a moment and it was as if she were playing back a cassette tape in her mind. She could hear her teacher telling them how to do the problems on the math paper, and she understood!

She interrupted her brother between numerator and denominator, "Oh Matthew, you're so pedantic."

That stopped him cold. "What does that mean?" he asked.

"I, I don't know!" she said. "Yes I do, it means bookish, academic…boring. Now let's see, six times four is twenty-four, so three fourths is eighteen twenty-fourths, five sixths is twenty twenty-fourths so five sixths is more than three-quarters. And, as for the improper fraction, twenty-nine fourths is seven and a quarter," she said with a big grin. "Let me see that paper." Carrie Lynn took the paper and re-figured the answers in about thirty seconds.

"There," she said, handing it back to Matthew, whose astonishment grew with every right answer.

"Well," he said pompously. "I guess I'm a better teacher than I thought."

"You sure are," Carrie Lynn said with a smirk, still not quite understanding what just happened.

"You'll be alright now," he said as he turned and left.

Carrie Lynn could hear him calling down the steps to their mom that he "straightened her out" with her math problems and she just smiled.

Something really weird's going on here, she thought as she started to get ready for bed.

FIVE

She awoke the next morning refreshed but kind of sorry she had such a dreamless sleep. She wouldn't have minded another dream like the one that Brat-yew interrupted the evening before. She heard her father in the kitchen, no doubt making coffee, as that was the very first thing he did every morning. She got up, went to the bathroom to brush her teeth, and then dressed for church. As she passed her mom's room she could hear her trying to decide which dress to wear.

"Let's see, the blue one with the white shoes or the print with the brown pumps?" Carrie Lynn heard her say.

"I like the blue one," she said as she walked by the door.

"Excuse me, dear?" her mom said.

"I said I like the blue one. It's always been my favorite."

"Why did you say that?"

"You were trying to pick a dress and I gave you my choice," Carrie Lynn said.

"Did I say that out loud?" Katherine asked.

"Sure, why else would I answer you?"

"I didn't think I said anything."

"Mom, you're losing it."

"I guess I am," she said.

Just then Dad came in carrying a cup of coffee for his wife. "Here you are honey," he said. "Just the way you like it."

"Thanks," said Katherine as she took a sip. *Ooh, it's a little too sweet*, she thought.

Carrie Lynn looked at her mom and that light went off in her head again. She *heard* her mom say that it was too sweet, but she didn't *say* anything at all!

"I'm the one who's losing it." Carrie Lynn was talking to herself as she continued down the hall. "I could have sworn that I heard Mom talking, but she didn't say anything. It's gotta be my imagination." She was shaking her head in disbelief as Matthew passed her on his way to his room.

"What's the matter with you?" he asked.

"Nothing."

"You look like you just saw a ghost," he said.

"No, maybe I just heard one," she replied.

"Uh, by the way you don't have any more Snickers do you?" Matthew asked with a grin.

"I might, but they're mine, Mom gave them to me for doing my science project and you can't have any 'cause you stole my other one," she said huffily.

He just stared at her. She looked back at him and that light went off again. She closed her eyes for a second, concentrated and when she opened them she heard him think, *I guess I'll just have to take one anyway.*

There was no doubt about it, she heard what he was thinking!

"Oh no you won't," she said indignantly.

"I won't what?" he asked.

35

"You won't take one anyway," she said, her hands on her hips.

"Take one what?"

"One of my Snickers," she said.

"I didn't say I would."

"I heard you *think it*!"

"Yeah, right!" he said.

"Yeah right," she said back. "Try me."

You are such a little wart! Matthew thought.

"And you are such a big jerk!" Carrie Lynn said out loud.

"Carrie Lynn!" her mother said. "I don't like that kind of talk."

"Mom, Carrie Lynn thinks she can read minds now!" said Matthew, laughing. "I told you she's goofy."

"I can, I just did," she said.

"A lucky guess," he said, laughing all the way down the hall.

"I really did, Mom. I don't know how, but I heard what Bratyew, I mean Matthew was thinking. I even heard you think that the coffee was too sweet, really!" Carrie Lynn said. "And, last night I could hear things, like you and Dad talking down stairs and Matthew on the phone. You gotta believe me."

"I do honey, I believe you."

"No you don't, you're just placating me."

"Placating you? Where did you get that word?" her mom asked.

"And, that's another thing, all of a sudden these words pop into my head."

"You mean like placate? Do you know what placate

means?"

"Yes, it means to sooth, or appease."

"Well that's right," said Mom. "Maybe it just means you have a naturally broad vocabulary."

"I don't know," Carrie Lynn said, even more confused.

"Hey, come on you guys," came Dad's voice. "Let's move it. You know how I hate to get to church after services start. And, by the way, the new door I put in on the porch doesn't close properly, I still have to adjust it, so keep an eye on Hazel."

"Ok," Mom and Carrie Lynn said together, as they each went about their ways, both shaking their heads.

One by one, they each left the house. Matthew first, so he could start up the van, Dad next, 'cause guys always seem to be ready before girls, and surprisingly enough, next came Mom (who was always last).

"Where is your daughter?" Michael asked, as he shooed Matthew out of the driver's seat.

"Deciding which dress she should wear," Katherine said.

Finally, Carrie Lynn appeared. She ran out the door and down the driveway. Michael opened the door for her but she ran back and made sure the new door was closed tight.

As they sat in the pew, waiting for the service to begin, Carrie Lynn did her best to be respectful and reticent, by not trying to hear other people's thoughts, but the temptation was too strong. Three rows up and two seats over sat Josh Sidwell with his mom and dad. Josh is Carrie Lynn's first crush. She and Kim sit in class and talk about Josh, and how cute he is. Kim doesn't know what Carrie Lynn sees in Josh, but it's fun to talk about boys anyway, even if they are still icky.

Carrie Lynn would love to find out if Josh felt the same way she did, so she closed her eyes and tried to concentrate in Josh's direction to see if she could hear what he was saying. After a moment, she saw the light and at first there was a rush of noisy voices all talking together, like the dial stuck between two different radio stations. The noise was too much and she had to turn it off. Then she tried to concentrate on Josh's thoughts. Again her senses were assailed with noise. "Everyone's thoughts!" she whispered to herself, smiling. She found that she could only do one super human feat at a time because hearing and reading thoughts together was just too much.

Then, as she concentrated a little harder in Josh's direction, a lady sat down and blocked her vision. Suddenly this woman's thoughts flooded Carrie Lynn's senses, *I hope service isn't too long*, she was thinking. *I've got a roast beef in the oven and I don't want it to overcook.*

Lady, I don't care about your roast beef, would you please hang up and put Josh on the line? Carrie Lynn thought, and then burst out laughing right there in church. Heads turned in her direction.

"Carrie Lynn, what's the matter with you?" Katherine said in a stage whisper.

"I'm sorry, Mom. I just thought something funny," she said.

"Well, this is neither the time nor the place for foolishness."

"I'm sorry!" Carrie Lynn snickered. Then she scooted over to get a better shot at Josh, and she tried again. It really was like a radio, she could kind of tune out the lady with the roast beef, and tune in Josh.

Boy, these pants sure do itch, he was thinking. *Why do I have to wear this stupid suit all the time? I hate wool!*

Josh's mom was saying something to him that she couldn't hear so she turned on her super hearing.

"…and stop fidgeting," she heard Josh's mom say.

Then she switched back to Josh's thoughts and heard him think, *You'd fidget too if you had to wear wool pants!*

Carrie Lynn laughed out loud again, and her mom looked at her as if to say, "If you don't settle down I'm going to kill you!"

This concentrating and switching back and forth was making her tired. She straightened up and composed herself for the rest of the service, checking in on Josh every once in a while only to hear how his "shoes hurt, or it's too hot in here, or his suit itches." *Listening to him is not very interesting*, Carrie Lynn thought, smiling to herself.

Before church was over, as Carrie Lynn listened the service, she absentmindedly tuned in on the pastor's thoughts. They were, with no surprise, exactly what he was saying to the congregation, word for word…except every now and then she thought she heard him think something about the *Yankees* and the *Mets*.

SIX

On the ride home, Carrie Lynn relaxed and was thinking how happy she was that her science project was done, her papers were gone over, and she had a whole bag of Snickers bars. Then she remembered how bratboy had threatened to "take one anyway," so she decided to read him. She closed her eyes, concentrated and then looked over in his direction and he noticed her staring at him, it made him think of that Snickers bar wrapper and how he was going to get one.

She heard him thinking of ways to find her hiding place. *Let's see, I can look under her bed, or inside her dresser, or…* Then all of a sudden, her reception started to break up, like when a cell phone goes out of range. She heard a lot of static, then his thoughts started to fade and she no longer could hear him.

"Where else are you gonna look?" she said to him, not thinking.

"What?" he said.

"Nothing," she said. Suddenly she decided to keep all this super hearing and mind reading stuff to herself…for now. Still she couldn't explain why she lost Matthew's signal, she tried to tune him in again, but nothing happened. She tried her dad, nothing. Then she concentrated on Mom, she knew she could hear her, but again no thoughts.

Was I imagining all this? Carrie Lynn thought. *No, it was real, at least I think it was. If it was real, what happened?*

When they got home, Carrie Lynn went to her room to change into her play clothes. While she was there she tried to think of what it was that caused that great change in her. She thought of all the things she'd done yesterday. She woke up, Dad was fixing breakfast but she didn't eat any. She went to her game and they won. She came back and did her experimenting, ate lunch and then she did her display. Then she went to her room and had a Snickers and Bratboy came in and they went over her papers.

"I know, Hazel was here!" she said quietly. "No, Hazel is always here." As she was trying to come up with something, she opened her closet door and got down the hatbox marked "Barbie clothes" just to check on her Snickers bars. Everything was there, her black glass kitten, her collection of rocks and minerals, her old coins that her grandfather had given her. There was the precious bag of Snickers, and some other trinkets, but nothing that could have caused her extra sensory perception.

"What was it?" she said as she put back the hatbox. She flopped down on the bed and thought some more, then she saw the book that she was reading for her book report.

"Oh well, I might as well read some more of this so I can write my report," she said as she picked up her book. She read the title: *Myths and Mysteries*, by Dr. Philip Wells.

"This not very interesting stuff," she said as she opened to the page she had marked with her ribbon and started to read.

...Still others say that they owed their abilities to the fact

that they used their brain to its fullest capacity. While modern man, it is said, uses only one tenth of his mental capability, the inhabitants of this island used all of theirs.

One writing on the subject of this island survived the fire and from it we learn that the people there were believed to have had a vast knowledge of plants and herbs…According to this source one of the reasons for their extraordinary power might have been something in their diet. They discovered that certain ingredients in a type of bread or cake they made gave them extra sensory abilities and they refined these to a point where they acquired almost super human capabilities. This is of course mostly legend, and impossible to prove, although there have been some reports…

Carrie Lynn jumped up and tried to absorb what she had just read. It was something about bread or cake that seemed important. She read out loud, "a type of bread or cake gave them extra sensory abilities. Cake…my crumb cake?"

She jumped up and hurriedly retrieved the hatbox. She routed through it, ignoring the Snickers, and dug until she found the Ziploc bag. She looked at the poor crumbled experiment that failed and said, "Nah, this couldn't have anything to do with it…"

She thought for a moment, and then remembered that eating the crumbs of this cake (that she almost threw away) was the very last thing she had done just before…

She quickly opened the bag and scooped another bit of the cake into her mouth. It was a little drier than before but again, that sweet taste. She thought what a shame that this cake was such a…

Wow! Here we go again! That flash of light and the dizziness and the sudden feeling that all of her senses were working twice as hard and sensing twice as much. This time though, it wasn't as frightening as before and, she paid more attention to what was going on. The sounds all started again, but she was able to control them. She heard Mom coming down the hall and zeroed in on her thoughts and heard her plans to mulch the flower beds out by the oak tree before it rained.

It was all back, and it must be the cake that does it, but how? She wondered if the other cakes might be able to do it too, but she would have to wait until Tuesday before she could try them. This was all too weird, if she didn't know better, she would swear it was a dream. But, it wasn't, it was all happening for real.

SEVEN

Carrie Lynn heard Matthew coming down the hall so she decided to check and see if she could "read" him again. She could, but all she could gather from the mumbling in his head was something about homework, lacrosse, calling Alex, and Snickers. She decided to check in on him every now and then just to make sure he wasn't planning to sneak into her room or anything.

Mom was getting ready to go outside, bratboy was going to call Alex, and Carrie Lynn was trying to understand what was going on.

"Carrie Lynn," she heard her mom call, "you want to help me outside for a while? Matthew is."

"Ok Mom," she said as she pulled on some shorts and a top and brushed her hair.

Michael was in the kitchen trying to decide what to do for breakfast. "Let's see, I could make creamed chipped beef, pancakes or just some bacon and eggs. But, I know what will happen, I'll make it and no one will want anything...I'll just have cereal."

Just then Katherine came through on her way outside. "Hi hon, what's for breakfast?" she asked.

"Well I..."

"A scrambled egg would be nice," she said as she gave him a hug and went out.

"Ok," he said.

Next, Matthew came through. "What'ya makin', Dad?" he asked.

"Your mom wants a scrambled egg."

"And could you make chipped beef to go with it?" he said almost pleading.

"I guess so," Michael said.

Matthew left and then it was Carrie Lynn's turn. As she came through carrying Hazel, Michael asked, "And, what would like this morning, missy?"

"Pancakes," she said, "blueberry pancakes. Ok Dad?"

I can't win, he thought.

Carrie Lynn heard him, and said, "Sure you can, Daddy."

"What was that?" he asked.

"I mean, I sure love your blueberry pancakes," she said, trying to change the subject. "You really are an epicurean."

"Thanks sweetie, an epicurean huh? Ok pancakes it is," he said, a little confused at the whole conversation. "Where 'ya going with Hazel?"

"Just on the porch, Mom asked me to brush her. She's leaving hair all over."

"Ok, I'll call you when everything's ready," Michael said.

"Ok, Dad."

Michael shook his head and thought, *When I fix something no one wants it, but when I don't fix anything everybody's hungry, go figure.*

Carrie Lynn heard his thoughts and smiled, but she didn't say anything this time. When she was finished with Hazel, she went out to help her mother. Matthew was already shoveling some mulch into a wheelbarrow. When it was full he lifted the handles to push it to the flower bed, but it was very heavy and he had to strain to keep it from tipping over.

"What's the matter, muscles, a little too heavy for you?" asked Carrie Lynn, with a smile.

"Don't you worry, half-pint, I can handle it," he groaned.

Carrie Lynn watched as he struggled to keep the wheelbarrow up. Just then Alex Williams came around the corner and saw Matthew too.

"Need a little help there, Matt?" he asked.

"No, I can handle it."

After what seemed a half an hour, Matthew was able to get the load to the flower bed where he dumped it and immediately sat down.

"Why didn't you have the man dump the mulch a little closer to the flower bed?" Matthew asked Katherine.

"And have him drive over my newly seeded lawn?" his mother answered. "No way!"

By then Carrie Lynn and Alex had walked the twenty feet or so from the mulch pile to the flower bed. "I've got an idea," Alex said to Matthew, as he pushed his glasses up on his nose. "I'll shovel the mulch and you drive it down hear, then you shovel it and I'll drive it."

"Alright."

"And don't put so much in, it'll be lighter," Mom added.

"Ok Mom," Matthew said.

And that's how it went for a while, the load was lighter but the pile wasn't getting much smaller. They decided to increase the load so it wouldn't take so long to finish. It was

Alex's turn to push the wheelbarrow, but because of the extra weight it was almost too heavy to lift. Matthew tried, but it was too much for him also. Carrie Lynn volunteered to heft the heavy weight herself, but the boys just laughed.

"You?" Matthew said. "Look munchkin, if Alex and I think it's heavy, how are you going to handle it?"

"Just watch," she said, as she wondered how she was ever going to push this wheelbarrow down to the flowers. She grabbed the handles and pulled up and put it right back down. Then she gave an extra effort closed her eyes and concentrated. There was the "bright light" and all of a sudden she could lift and turn the wheelbarrow as if it were empty! She started to move it down to the flower bed when Josh Sidwell, Carrie Lynn's boyfriend, came riding in on his bike.

"Hi," Josh said to Carrie Lynn.

"Hi," she said.

"I saw you at church."

"I saw you too. I bet you couldn't wait to get out of that itchy suit, could you?" Carrie Lynn asked, all innocent like.

"Boy, you know it!" Josh said. Then he thought about what Carrie Lynn asked. He let it go and asked if he could help.

"Sure," she said. "Can you push this down to the end of the house while I go help Mom?"

"Ok," he said.

"Right," Alex said. "I'd like to see you move that thing down to that flower bed."

"Me too," Matthew added half kidding.

"Ok," Josh said as he walked over and lifted, or tried to

lift, the wheelbarrow. He was struggling with the weight and the other boys were starting to giggle and laugh. Carrie Lynn didn't like them making fun of him so she concentrated hard on the wheelbarrow, saw the light, and Josh suddenly lifted it with no effort!

"Wow!" she said to herself.

Josh moved the load as if there was nothing in the wheelbarrow. The boys couldn't believe their eyes.

"Where would you like this, Mrs. Foster?" Josh asked nonchalantly.

"Right there would be fine Josh, thanks," said Katherine amazed.

"Le'me try that," said Alex as he went down and lifted the wheelbarrow. He grunted and strained but could barely get it off of the ground.

"How'd you do that?" he asked.

"It's easy, watch," Josh went over and with Carrie Lynn's help again lifted it with no effort at all.

"I don't believe it," said Matthew.

"Believe it, Hercules," Carrie Lynn said. "You and Alex go rest a while, Josh and I will finish the job."

"No problem," said Alex.

"Let me try that," Matthew said. "If Josh can do it I know I can."

He grabbed the handles, with a defiant look on his face. He groaned and grunted and his face turned red, but he was determined to get that load down to the flowers. As he was finally able to lift it off of the ground, Carrie Lynn got an idea. She thought she'd give Matthew a little help. As he leaned forward and pushed with all his strength, she concentrated on the wheelbarrow and it was suddenly very light. Both Matthew and the wheelbarrow shot forward, passed the flower bed by about ten feet and spilled on the lawn, Matthew tumbling after it. This caused the other children to fall down laughing.

"Matthew will you stop fooling around and try to be more careful!" Katherine said, trying not to break up herself.

"But Mom, I…it…the…" Matthew stammered.

"Way to go, Superman," Carrie Lynn snickered.

"Ok, start cleaning it up," Katherine said.

Just then Michael called from the porch, "Come and get it!"

"Saved by the bellow," said Mom with a laugh.

"Huh, what's that mean?" Matthew said.

"Never mind, Matt, it's way over your head," Carrie Lynn said.

"Oh yeah?"

"Yeah!"

"What's it mean then?" he asked.

"It's an old expression taken from boxing. The real saying is saved by the bell, but Mom made a joke out of it and said, 'Saved by the bell-ow', meaning to cry out or yell, get it?" Carrie Lynn explained. "Right Mom?"

"That's right, honey," Katherine said, a little bewildered.

Carrie Lynn thought that she was saved by the bell too because all of this intense concentrating was very tiring. She decided to try it a little at a time only when it was necessary. After all she didn't want to waste it.

Dad had everything all set on the picnic table but didn't know Josh and Alex were joining them. "Have you guys had any breakfast?" he asked.

"I have," Josh said.

"I haven't," said Alex.

"Pancakes, eggs or chipped beef?" Michael asked.

"That sounds good," Alex said.

They all sat down to eat and were passing plates and asking each other if they wanted this or that. As they ate they carried on their little conversations. Mom was taking to Dad and Carrie Lynn was asking Josh about something and Alex was teasing Matthew about something. Everyone was trying to be heard above everyone else and it got louder and louder until the little group of six people sounded a lot like lunchtime at school. Michael couldn't hear what Katherine was saying and Alex was shouting at Matthew to be heard until finally Michael realized that it was all too loud and in a voice that could be heard over everyone else he said, "Quiet!"

Suddenly there was silence. Everyone looked over at Dad, their mouths agape. "What is everyone talking about?" he asked with a smile.

They all looked at each other for a moment not knowing what to say. No one knew what the others were talking about except of course Carrie Lynn who piped right up and had complete answers. She had, after all, been listening with a little extra sensory help.

"Well," she began. "Mom was asking you about planting a new tree in the back yard to provide more shade and you said fine, as long as it wasn't too close to the power lines. Josh was telling me about how he and his dad did his science project out in back yard growing mushrooms and Alex was telling Matthew how Josh was able to move the wheel barrow down to the flower bed all by himself, but he hasn't really got any idea how he did it. And, could I have some more eggs—please?" They all looked at each other in amazement.

"How did you know all that?" Katherine asked.

"I was just listening," she said with a smile.

EIGHT

"Michael!" Katherine screamed from the back porch into the kitchen were he was cleaning up the dishes. Carrie Lynn was following behind.

Startled and almost dropping a pan of water on the floor he said, "What!"

"I've got worms!" she said.

"I told you not to eat raw pork chops," Michael said wryly.

"Very funny! No, I've got tent worms look," she said as she held out her hand to show a green caterpillar.

"Look out, he may bite you," he said.

"They only eat green things," she replied.

"Better watch out for your thumb then. You know how you always say you've got a *green one*! Ha ha ha!" Michael laughed out loud. Carrie Lynn laughed too.

"Oh, you are just full of jokes today aren't you?" Katherine said, not at all amused.

"And what are you laughing at, missy?" she said to Carrie Lynn.

"Mom just give them a little dose of malathion it should do the trick," Carrie Lynn said still giggling from Dad's joke.

"Malathion huh?" Katherine said. "What do you know about malathion?"

"I know it's good for tent worms, or is it bad for tent worms? Any way if you don't have malathion, rotenone will do just fine," she said as she went back out side.

Katherine waited until Carrie Lynn was out of hearing range (or so she thought) and then said, "Michael, that girl is starting to worry me. She's been acting awfully strange lately. Do you know what she said to me earlier? I thought she was just playing at the time but now I'm not so sure."

"What are you talking about?" Michael asked.

"This morning she answered a question, I didn't even ask, about which dress I was going to wear to church. And she's been using some awfully big words lately like placate and malathion and..."

"Epicurean," Michael interrupted. "Yes I know. Earlier she called me an epicurean."

"Do you know what I think?" she asked, then answering her own question, "I think we may have a genius on our hands."

"Kathy, I love our daughter very much and I think she's a bright intelligent and maybe a very intuitive girl, but I don't think she's quite a genius. We had to get Matthew to help her with her math remember?"

"Yes, but did you see how quickly she caught on?"

"And, do you think she can really answer questions before you ask them?" Michael said with a skeptical tone.

Katherine said, "Maybe she's a genius with language, you heard the words she was using. At first I thought that she just had a good vocabulary, but now I'm not so sure. And maybe she's psychic!"

"Well let's just keep an eye on her and see what happens," Michael said, humoring her and returning to his dishes.

Katherine went back outside and joined Carrie Lynn and Josh who were still working with the mulch. Carrie Lynn was filling the wheelbarrow and Josh was pushing it down to the flower bed. Matthew and Alex were nowhere to be seen as the work must have gotten boring for them and they found other things to do.

"You two are really doing a great job," Katherine said. "What do you say, when we finish, we run up to Patterson's for some ice cream?"

"Great!"

"Thanks Mom!" the two workers said together.

Katherine went back to her gardening, but every now and then she couldn't help but glance over at Carrie Lynn. She didn't know what she expected her to do, but she just had to keep and eye on her anyway. She didn't contemplate her *flying* or anything like that although she probably could have!

An hour or so later, when they had finished, Katherine drove Josh and Carrie Lynn up to Patterson's Deli for the ice cream. Michael didn't go because he had some chores that Katherine had left for him but they promised to bring him something. As they were looking over the menu, Katherine decided to give Carrie Lynn a test to see if maybe she was a little psychic.

"Let me see which one do I want?" she said out loud, then concentrated real hard on the two items that she would like to have, hoping Carrie Lynn would read her thoughts and tell her which one she would like to have. She looked out of the corner of her eye to see if there was any reaction from Carrie Lynn who was just staring up at the menu on the wall. Katherine tried again. "Which one do I want?" she said again a little louder this time and concentrated, still no reaction from the girl. What Katherine didn't know was that all Carrie Lynn had on her mind at that moment was ice cream and all the concentrating in the world couldn't get her mind off of that.

As they sat in the booth eating, Katherine asked Josh how his science project was going.

"I'm done," he said. "It's on mushrooms and how to make them grow. My dad helped me grow some in my yard. He likes mushrooms, I mean the kind you eat."

"Yuck, I think they're terrible," said Carrie Lynn.

"Me too," said Josh. "But they make a great science project. Boy once you get them to grow they just don't stop. We started in one corner of my mom's garden and now they're growing all over. My mom's not too happy."

"Can you eat them though?" Katherine asked.

"I think you can, but Mom doesn't like them either," Josh said with a laugh.

"By the way, you two have a geography quiz tomorrow don't you?"

"Yes Mom!" Carrie Lynn said, in a ho hum kind of voice knowing what was coming next.

"Well have you studied?" she asked.

"I'm supposed to tonight," Josh said.

"Don't worry Mom, I think I'm going to do just fine on that 'ole geography quiz tomorrow," Carrie Lynn said confidently. She had a plan. The quiz was going to be one where Mrs. Collison asks the questions out loud and the kids write down the answers. If she has trouble with a question she will simply read the teacher's thoughts for the answer. So she was sure she didn't have to worry about studying tonight. Of course she will only use this in an emergency.

"I know you will, honey," Katherine said knowing she will do well because her little girl just may be a genius!

NINE

On the trip home the two kids sat in the back seat of the van carrying ice cream for the others. They brought Dad a chocolate sundae with nuts and Matthew and Alex got a one-scoop cone each. The ride was a pleasant one for Katherine, with Carrie Lynn and Josh so full of ice cream, there wasn't the chatter and laughing that usually accompanies a journey with ten-year-olds. When they pulled into the driveway they saw Alex and Matthew riding their bikes in the street. Matthew rode up to the driver's side of the van and said in a questioning statement, "Dad said you guys went for ice cream?"

"Yes we did," Katherine said.

"Did you get me any?"

"Maybe."

"Yes!" he said. "What about Alex?"

"Him too."

"All right!" Matthew said, his mouth already watering.

Katherine got out and opened the back door of the van. The kids got out with the card board trays they were carrying with the ice cream in them. Carrie Lynn gave each of the boys their cones.

"This is it?" Matthew asked. "One scoop!"

"This is fine, Mrs. Foster. Thanks," said Alex.

"You're welcome, Alex, and thank you for your help," Katherine said.

"Only one scoop?!" Matthew asked.

"A," Katherine counted. "I wasn't sure you two would even be here when we got back. "B, Carrie Lynn and Josh worked real hard on the mulch and they deserved a treat. And C, you did about a one-scoop job seeing as how I had to clean up the mulch you spilled on the lawn."

"Ha, ha," Carrie Lynn said. And, in her sing song voice she sang, "We ha-ad sun-daes."

Matthew saw red and said, "You know what I'd like to do? I'd like to put this right in your..." As he said this he acted like he was going to push the one scoop cone into his sister's face. Carrie Lynn saw it coming and didn't know Matthew was only kidding. She didn't stop to think but reacted in the only way she could. She covered her face and concentrated on pushing the menacing ice cream cone away. It worked! Suddenly Matthew felt like something grabbed his hand. The cone jerked away from Carrie Lynn, came right back at the surprised Matthew and hit him squarely in the nose. Everyone fell down laughing again. Everyone that is except Carrie Lynn who didn't see anything due to the fact that she had her face covered. When she finally did see what had happened she couldn't help but laugh too.

"Did you see that?" an embarrassed Matthew said as he wiped cookie dough ice cream from his face. "She did that on purpose!"

"She didn't do anything," Katherine said, her eyes starting to tear up from laughter. "I saw the whole thing."

"I saw it too, Matt," Alex said holding his stomach. "You did it to yourself!"

"But…I…it…must have slipped," Matthew stammered again. It just wasn't his day. Josh, trying not to laugh too hard, offered him some of the napkins they brought from the deli. As he was cleaning up, Michael came over and asked what was so funny.

"Oh, you missed it," Katherine said. Just talking about it got her started laughing again. "Your son hit himself in the face with his ice cream cone."

"Why'd you do that, son?" Michael asked Matthew.

"Oh, I didn't have anything else to do," he said.

"Here, Mr. Foster," Josh said as he handed Michael his almost melted Chocolate sundae.

"Thank you, Josh," Michael said. "I'll tell you what, Matthew," he continued, "you can have mine."

"No thanks, Dad."

"No really you can have it."

"Ok, thanks," Matthew said as he went off into the house to wash his face.

The rest of the day was pretty uneventful. Michael made a late lunch of hot dogs and beans. Josh and Alex stayed for something to eat but then Alex went home before the rain, which was predicted for that afternoon, finally arrived. Everyone else went inside except Katherine, who as usual, stayed out working until the very last minute and still managed to get pretty soaked before finally deciding to come in.

Hazel meowed to go outside but when Carrie Lynn opened the door to let her, she took one look at the weather and promptly changed her mind.

"What's the matter, Hazie, don't like the mean 'ole rain?" Carrie Lynn asked. Hazel backed up like a tractor-trailer and retreated to her favorite spot under Mom and Dad's bed.

Matthew went to his room and put on one of his CDs, while Carrie Lynn and Josh went down stairs to play. "What do you want to do?" Carrie Lynn asked. "We have videos."

Josh looked over their collection of tapes. "Oh, you have the *Wizard of Oz*," he said.

"Yeah."

"I've seen it a hundred times."

"Me too, hey want to play a game? We have checkers, Parcheesi, Clue, Sorry…"

"Sorry's ok," Josh said, and Carrie Lynn went to get the game. While she was away, Josh noticed her science project over in the corner and went over to have a look. "Hey this is really good," he said admiring her work.

Carrie Lynn came back carrying the game. "Thanks, Mom and Dad helped me with the display but I did all the baking myself," she said.

"Wow look at them, this one's pretty high and this one's just a pancake."

"That's the whole idea, I wanted to show how you make a cake rise. But, you should have seen the one that got messed up!" she said, then caught herself. If she told Josh about her crumb cake should she tell him about the special powers it has? She wanted to tell someone, because the secret was driving her crazy. She tried to tell her family but they didn't believe her. She wasn't sure she wanted to tell them anyway, but could she trust Josh?

"What about it?" Josh asked.

"What about what?" Carrie Lynn asked.

"What about the one that got messed up?"

She decided to tell him.

Just like they do in the movies Carrie Lynn looked left and then right to see if anyone was listening. She moved closer to Josh and said, "If I tell you a secret, will you promise not to say anything to anyone?"

Suddenly the atmosphere turned serious. "I promise," he said.

Then Carrie Lynn told him the whole story. The crumby cake, the sounds, the mind reading, the incident in church, the fun with the wheel barrow and the ice cream cone—all of it. The only thing she didn't tell him was that there was a little bit of the cake left.

Josh didn't know what to think. He just sat there trying to take it all in. "You mean you actually heard me say my suit was too itchy?" he asked.

"You didn't say it," Carrie Lynn said. "You thought it."

"Ey yai yai," he said. "I better watch what I think!"

"I can only do it when people are close by, if they are too far away it doesn't work," she said.

"And you actually made the wheelbarrow lighter just by thinking about it?"

"Yeah, it's one of the things I discovered by accident that I can do."

"Can you do something now? I mean like move something?"

"I can try," Carrie Lynn said. "Watch the Sorry box."

She concentrated on the game for a while and saw the

bright light in her mind. Slowly it began to move! She slid it across the table in Josh's direction. He reached out to stop it before it fell off the edge. Skeptical, he picked it up and turned it up side down examining it from all sides. Then he looked under the table for wires or anything she might use to make it move, he saw nothing.

"Is this a trick?" he asked, looking at her sideways.

"Nope."

"You really did it," he said. "You really did it!"

"Yep."

She concentrated again and slowly it rose from the table! She spun the box around in mid air and Josh's mouth fell open. He put his hands over the spinning box and waved them back and forth expecting to feel wires or something, but again nothing. Suddenly it was harder and harder for her to keep it suspended. She concentrated, but the light was getting dimmer and dimmer. The box began to sink and she really had to strain to keep it up. Then, as if somebody pulled the plug, the box fell, spilling the game board, cards and colored game pieces all over the floor.

"Why'd you do that?" Josh asked surprised at the mess.

"It just slipped," Carrie Lynn said. But, what she didn't say was that her powers were fading already. The room brightened as the rain drifted off and the sun came out again, but neither of the kids noticed.

"And you can read people's thoughts too! Wow!" said Josh as he started to pick up the pieces of the game.

"That's what I'm going to do tomorrow during the quiz. When I don't know an answer I'll just concentrate on what Mrs. Collisons thinking."

"Isn't that cheating?" Josh asked.

"Well, kinda' but I'm only using it for insurance. My Friday papers weren't too good last week, and Mom wasn't too happy," Carrie Lynn said.

"Why don't you just study?"

"Oh I will, this is just in case."

The phone rang and a moment later Michael called down from the top of the steps.

"Josh, your mom's on the phone."

"Ok," he said. He picked up the down stairs phone and talked to his mother a minute, then turned to Carrie Lynn and started to say something.

She interrupted and said, "You've got to go."

"Yeah", Josh said. "Did you read my mind?"

"No, I just guessed," she said. She saw him to the door but before he left she said, "Remember don't tell anybody anything."

"I won't, I promise."

"Ok, see you tomorrow," she said. And for the rest of the night she didn't try any extraordinary things, which disappointed her mother who expected her to. She did study her geography notes, sort of, but she was tired and didn't put a lot of work into it. She wasn't worried about it though, because there was always the other way to pass the test. She decided to save the last little bit of the crumb cake until tomorrow morning...no need to waste it on anything tonight.

TEN

She heard gentle knocking on her door and her dad popped his head in to wake her. "Come on, sunshine, it's time to get up. It's the start of a brand new week and you've got the world by the tail!" Carrie Lynn just moaned and pulled the covers over her head. Her dad was one of those people who always woke up in a good mood and she was not a morning person. "I'll give you five minutes and then I'm coming back to get you," he said as he went next door to wake Matthew.

Seven minutes later he was back but Carrie Lynn was up and almost dressed. "That's my girl," he said. "Want some cereal?"

"Ok," she said as she went off to the bathroom to wash and brush her hair. She ate her cereal had a glass of orange juice and gathered her books into her back pack. Matthew was out at the bus stop, her father was gone and her mother was making her bed.

"Did you brush your teeth?" Katherine asked.

"Yes Mom."

"Don't forget your lunch."

"No Mom."

"You better hurry, your bus will be out there in five

minutes," Katherine said.

"Ok Mom," she said. Morning was the only time of day that Carrie Lynn was economical with words. She kissed her mom and started out to the bus stop when she realized she had forgotten her cake. "Holy smoke!" she yelled and ran to her room and almost pushed her mom out of the way to get to the closet door.

"What's the problem?" Katherine asked.

"I almost forgot my cake," she said.

"Your cake?"

"I mean my Snickers, I was going to take one for lunch."

"Ok honey, gee."

Carrie Lynn hurriedly took down the hatbox and rummaged through everything until she found the plastic bag with the cake crumbs. She took them out and closed the hatbox lid.

"I thought you wanted a Snickers?" Katherine asked.

"Oh yeah! I forgot," she said in a "silly me" kind of voice. She opened the box, took out a Snickers and practically threw the hat box marked Barbie clothes back up on the top shelf of her closet. "Bye Mom," she said as she ran off to meet the bus just in time.

Once in her seat she opened the Ziploc bag and scooped out the last of the cake into her hand. *Not much left*, she thought as she carefully placed every available crumb into her mouth. She even shook what was left in the bag in there too. This time though, it was drier than the last time. She ate all she could and waited. It took a while, but finally there was the flash of light. Not as bright as before but there it was. *Good*, she thought. She hoped the rest of her cakes weren't drying out too badly, just in case they were "special" like this one was. She thought she'd try out her talents.

Kate Miller was sitting in the seat in front of her. She wondered what Kate had on her mind. *Peanut butter and jelly! Another peanut butter and jelly sandwich!* Kate was thinking as she was looking in her lunch bag. *I wish I could buy lunch today.*

Kate just happened to look back at Carrie Lynn who smiled and asked, "You know what they're having for lunch today? Burritos! I sure am glad I brought."

"Wow, me too," Kate said. And Carrie Lynn smiled to herself.

Things started out as usual in Carrie Lynn's class, Mrs. Collison passed out a sheet with their spelling words for the week. They study them and then on Friday they have a spelling/vocabulary test. Carrie Lynn always does well on her test, thanks in no small part to her mother's practicing with her all week. This time though as they went over them in class, she found if she just concentrated, she could record them in her mind. Kind of like regular studying only ten times better. All she had to do was think of a word and she could play back the recording exactly as she learned it. This is how she knew all those big words. If she thought of a word (or a definition) that she heard before, her subconscious mind would automatically play it back for her conscious mind. She'd use the word correctly and, didn't even know how it was happening.

She chuckled to herself. *This is great*! she thought. *Studying's a breeze this way, I wish I could always study like this.*

By the time they were finished going over their words Carrie Lynn had them memorized forever. For the next two hours everything they talked about or studied was permanently stored in her mind. She was concentrating away and getting smarter by the minute. She felt as if she were suddenly using more of her brain.

During lunch, she sat with Kim and Chloe and took a break from concentrating. She just talked and enjoyed her ham, lettuce and tomato sandwich. Josh sat at another table with the boys but every now and then he took a look over at her and she glanced back at him. They didn't say anything to each other but the looks they gave spoke loudly of the secret they shared.

After recess, back in class they talked a little about tomorrow's science fair and got last minute details about where they were to take their projects. "First, second, and third grades are to bring their projects to the library," Mrs. Collison told them. "And fourth and fifth grades are to go to the multi purpose room. Judging will be tomorrow afternoon. Parents can come to the fair tomorrow afternoon from five until eight o'clock and all day Wednesday. Winners will be officially announced on Wednesday and projects can be picked up anytime Thursday. Everything has been explained in detail in the science fair letter sent out earlier, but are there any questions you have about the fair?" No one raised a hand. "Good, and I can't wait to see your projects. Now let's get ready for our geography quiz." Groans from the class. "As usual this will be like our other quizzes. I will ask the questions and you will write down the answers. The quiz will be on our continents. All answered correctly will be an A, one wrong, a B, two a C and so on."

For the first time in a while Carrie Lynn was absolutely confident they she would ace this one! She looked over her left shoulder at Josh who was talking to a boy beside him. He saw her looking at him, smiled and gave her the crossed fingers sign. She gave him the clenched fist sign back and Mrs. Collison got out the test. She passed out a stack of answer sheets to the first child in each row who took one and passed them back to the student behind. There was rustling as the class got out their pencils.

Carrie Lynn turned on her extra sensory switch and got ready for the quiz. She told herself she would only use her powers if she got into trouble.

"Now everyone, I will ask the question once and you will have one minute to answer, then we move on to the next question. If you don't understand or don't hear me properly I will ask it a second time, but only if I have to, understand?" Everyone nodded. "There are ten questions so we should be all through with the quiz in about fifteen minutes. Then after we grade them, if we have time, we can watch a video on the continents and how they were formed. It's very interesting and I think you will enjoy it very much. Now everyone ready? Oh, I forgot, here is a map of the world showing an outline of the continents, but you'll notice there are no names on them. You'll have to use your brains and remember what we studied in class. If you studied at home I'm sure you'll all do well. Ok, number one, four of the seven continents begin with the letter A, name them."

Maurice Simpson, one of those children who always shouts out and can't seem to keep still, announced, "Oh, I know that one."

Carrie Lynn smiled and started to write. Africa, Asia, Australia, and...and...America ? *That's not right*, she thought. She tried to bring up the answer from her subconscious, but she was getting too much information all at the same time and it was confusing her. *I'll see what Mrs. Collison's thinking.*

Mrs. Collison, the good teacher that she is, was trying to *will* the students to do well and was saying the answers over and over in her mind hoping they could some how pick up her thoughts. If only she knew that at least one of her students was doing just that! Carrie Lynn was receiving her loud and clear. *Africa, Asia, Antarctica...*

Antarctica, that's it! Hee, hee, hee. She chuckled to herself as she wrote down the answer. *This is too easy.*

"Ok, number two," the teacher went on. "Our country is in which continent?"

"Got this one," Maurice declared.

Carrie Lynn knew this one too, and wrote down North America. *So far so good*, she thought.

"Ok everyone?" the teacher asked. "Number three, two other large countries share our continent, what are they?"

Ok, um, Mexico and...and... Carrie Lynn frowned tapping her pencil on her desk. Then she tuned in on Mrs. Collison again, who was humming the answers in her head. *Mex-i-co and Ca...(static)... (static)...Mexi...(static)...and Can...*

Whoa, what's the matter? Carrie Lynn thought. *Oh no! It can't stop now!* Then she tried again and heard the teacher sing, *Can-a-da.*

Whew, That was close. I hope the rest are easy! she thought as she wrote the answer.

"Number four, which continent has been referred to as the Dark Continent? Remember we talked about the explorers and how they were afraid of the dense jungles."

"Yeah, jungles with the lions."

"That'll do, Maurice!" Mrs. Collison said.

"Oh!" Carrie Lynn said out loud, and quickly put her hand up to her mouth. She looked back at Josh again who was writing an answer. He looked up and saw her and she gave him a wink, something she had never done to a boy before. She turned around and wrote "Africa" on the sheet.

After about a minute, Mrs. Collison said, "Number five, half way there, and I know you all are doing just fine!" All the children smiled. "Ok, here's a tuffy, what separates the continent of Asia from the continent of Europe?"

"What?" Carrie Lynn whispered out loud. "I don't remember this!" She tried her subconscious again, and all she got was scrambled information. She turned to Mrs. Collison's thoughts again, and she heard, "The...(more static) mount...(static).

Oh man, why is it stopping so soon? Carrie Lynn pleaded, *I have to get this answer.* But, all she could get from her sources was garbled information. She tried hearing her teacher's thoughts, she tried hearing her classmates' whisperings, she tried her subconscious, but nothing was working. She stared at the blank number five and wanted to write something, but as hard as she tried, she could not come up with an answer.

"Number six and number seven."

"Ohhhh!" she said under her breath.

"Name the largest and the smallest continents," Mrs. Collison said. "Put the largest one on number six and the smallest on number seven."

Ok, Carrie Lynn said to herself. *The smallest is Australia, I know that.* She wrote the answer on the seventh line. *But the largest, I thought was Africa, but I don't think she would put another Africa answer so soon after the Dark Continent question. So what is it?* She thought for a moment then she looked up from her paper at Mrs. Collison. She closed her eyes and really concentrated hard this time. She saw the light again but it was very dim. Squeezing her eyes tight, she began to see it grow brighter until she could hear Mrs. Collison's thoughts again just in time to hear her think *Asia*.

"Thank you!" the girl said and she made a promise that she would never try to use this way to pass a test ever again.

"Number eight, what is the only other continent that we could visit by car? All others we would have to fly or take a boat trip to. I'll give you a hint, it's not Australia." There was some laughter from the class as the children started to write their answers. Carrie Lynn looked up at the map and recognized the United States and knew that it was North America. She saw the large continent to the south connected by a thin strip of land and knew this must be the only continent she could drive to. And that other continent must be South America. She wrote it down.

"Number nine," the teacher said. "Which continent is always cold even in the summer time?"

Oh I know this...Arctica, Carrie Lynn said as she wrote down her answer quickly. She looked around at the others wondering how anyone could miss that one.

When Mrs. Collison saw that the children were finished writing she asked the final question. "Ok, our last question…this wasn't too hard was it?" There was a mixed reaction in the class. "Come on, I know you all did very well. Number ten, Europe and Asia are sometimes considered as one continent and they refer to this one continent as…what?"

"I got this one," Maurice announced and started to scratch the answer on his paper.

I wish I did, Carrie Lynn thought. *If only the crumb cake hadn't worn off so soon. If only I had studied harder!*

Mrs. Collison was humming *Eurasia* over and over again, but those who knew the answer were already writing it down and those who didn't, weren't picking up her transmissions, even the one who really could a few minutes ago!

Carrie Lynn looked back at Josh. He had just written his answer and caught her looking at him again. He smiled as if to say everything's going good and she gave back a nervous grin that she hoped said the same thing. But, she was worried.

"Ok, everybody, time's up. Please exchange papers with the neighbor in front of you and we'll see how everybody did," Mrs. Collison said. Carrie Lynn wished she had something to write on the lines next to the numbers ten and five, but there was nothing she could think of to write. She reluctantly passed her paper to Virginia who was waiting to exchange papers with her.

Mrs. Collison announced the answers one by one and the children either cheered or groaned when they heard them.

Carrie Lynn was sure she had done well on all of the answers but five and ten. When she heard that it was mountains that divided Europe from Asia, she could have kicked herself. *Now I remember!* she thought. But when the teacher said that the continent that was always cold was Ant-arctica she froze. *I wrote Arctica, not Antarctica...maybe Virginia won't notice.*

Just then Virginia raised her hand. "Mrs. Collison, what if someone wrote Arctica instead of Antarctica?" Carrie Lynn's heart started beating faster.

"Well, the answer is Antarctica," she said, and paused a long moment. Carrie Lynn's heart beat faster still. "What do you think, class? Is Arctica close enough?" Now Carrie Lynn's heart stopped all together.

"Yeah," the majority of children proclaimed, and her heart started again.

"Whew!"

Then she learned that Eurasia is the name they call the combined continents of Europe and Asia. *I knew that too!* she thought. *If only I hadn't put all of my trust in my powers and just thought about the answers...*

As it turned out, she got a C on the quiz, although it could have been worse. After school Josh, who got an A, wanted to know how she did.

"Well, not too good, I got a C."

"How come?" he asked.

"Everything went wrong, you were right I should have just studied more," she said.

"Don't feel too bad," Josh said. "I graded Maurice's paper, and he got a D!" They both laughed, but Carrie Lynn wasn't happy. Now she was going to have to have to explain another bad quiz grade in this week's Friday folder!

ELEVEN

The rest of the day Carrie Lynn tried using her powers, but nothing seemed to work. Even when she tried really hard, the best she could accomplish was a very dim light and some garbled voices coming from who knows where. She couldn't even tell if she was hearing people's words or reading their thoughts. She couldn't wait until the science fair was over so she could try the rest of her cakes to see if they had the power. But she had mixed emotions on the subject. While it was fun reading people's thoughts and moving things around, she was afraid that this whole thing might eventually get her into trouble, as it almost had with her quiz.

So at least for now she concentrated on nothing but the science fair. She liked seeing all the projects and although it was hard work, she enjoyed doing hers because she did it all by herself. *Who knows maybe I'll be a scientist someday*, she thought.

She was up in her room when she heard her mother calling her to dinner. "Come and get it!" she called up the stairs. "Get it while it's hot."

Carrie Lynn wasn't sure, but from the aroma it smelled like chili and corn bread, one of her favorites.

Matthew hit the kitchen door at the same time she did and tried to muscle his way in before she could. "That one's mine," he said, pointing to a steaming bowl of chili with melted cheese on top.

"Ok, I don't care which one you have. I just want to sit next to Dad," Carrie Lynn said, through clenched teeth.

"Alright, alright. Can we have a meal without you two going at each other the whole time?" Michael asked.

"Well, he practically knocked me down getting in here," Carrie Lynn said.

"It was an accident," Matthew explained.

"Yeah, sure it was! You just wanted the biggest bowl of chili," she said. "And, you better not get any ideas about going into my room either."

"I wasn't anywhere near your room."

"You know if I didn't know better, I'd swear you two were brother and sister," Michael said trying to calm the situation.

"I wish I didn't have a brother."

"Or a sister."

"Oh, you two say that now, but in a few short years you will love each other very very much," said Michael with an exaggerated sweetness.

They looked at each other and both said, "Bleech! No Way!"

Michael laughed out loud and asked Matthew to pass the salad.

"Well, tomorrow's the big day, huh?" Mom said to Carrie Lynn. "I think you've got a good shot for a ribbon at the fair. I can't wait to see all the projects. We'll take a ride over to the school tomorrow evening to see them, ok?"

"Ok," she said and they ate the rest of their meal in relative calmness.

Just before Carrie Lynn went to sleep that evening, she read the rest of her book and decided how she was going to do her book report. The teacher explained that they could write their report as a news story or as if they were one of the characters in the book. She decided to write it as if she were one of the people on the island, and explain what it was like to have the powers they had. Why not? She knew exactly how it was!

She finished the book and tossed it on the floor. She slipped out of bed, opened her door and called out, "Good night."

From her parents' room she heard her mom say, "Good night, honey."

And, from down stairs she heard her dad call, "Nighty night."

Carrie Lynn got back in bed, set her alarm clock, turned off her light and settled down to sleep. She thought about how she was going to write her paper as she drifted off.

Suddenly she felt the whole house start spinning around. She opened her eyes and looked out the window. There were dark gray clouds everywhere and everything looked as if it were in black and white, with no color anywhere. She could hear the wind howling. As she watched the clouds roll across the sky, she saw Matthew and Alex ride by on their bikes and look in the window. Alex waved and pushed his glasses up. Matthew pulled out a Snickers bar and grinned at her as he started eating it.

"Hey!" Carrie Lynn shouted, but he and Alex just raced off. She ran to the front door and tried to chase after them, but the house was spinning so fast that she was afraid to go outside. *This is weird!* she thought. Then, as the house turned, she saw her mom out in the back yard planting flowers.

"Hi, honey," she said. "Want to help me with the mulch?"

"Yes Mom, but I can't get out! The house is spinning too fast!"

"Ok, dear," Katherine said.

"But, Mom!" Carrie Lynn said as the house revolved and her mom drifted out of view. "This is *really* weird!" she said out loud.

Then Josh Sidwell walked by pushing a wheelbarrow.

"Josh, can you help me? I can't come outside, the house won't stop turning."

Josh cupped his hands around his mouth and shouted against the wind, "Why don't you just concentrate and make it stop."

"That's a good idea," she said, and she tried really hard to make the house stop. She concentrated with all her might until she saw the light and the house started to slow down. She had her power back! She kept thinking real hard until it stopped completely. All at once everything was very still.

She opened the door and stepped out into a very strange land. Suddenly everything burst into color, dayglow bright fluorescent color. There were tall golden buildings, an azure blue sky and people in brightly colored clothes that looked like they were from some ancient time long ago, friendly people who waved and said, "Hello, Hi, Carrie Lynn."

She waved and said, "Hello," back to them.

As she ventured out a little further she could see other buildings in gleaming white marble. And lights, bright lights illuminating everything. "This is a very nice place," she said to herself.

And then she heard someone say, "Thank you. It is a very nice place isn't it?" That caught her off guard for a second until she realized she could hear all of them talking and saying hello, and they could hear her, but they weren't speaking. They were communicating with their minds. She also noticed that they weren't really walking but sort of floating along. Not quite flying, but not really walking either.

"I wonder how they're doing that?" she thought.

"We just *wish* ourselves to glide, and we do," a very nice man replied to her.

"Is that what you call it, gliding?" she asked.

"Yes, can't you do it? I see you have the ability to read thoughts. You probably could glide yourself."

"I, I never tried," Carrie Lynn said and she wished (concentrated), and found herself gliding too. "I can do it!"

"Of course you can, you know the secret," the man said.

"What secret?" the girl asked, eyes wide with wonder.

"The secret of the cake. If you know how to make the cake, you have the secret, and you must know how to make the cake or you couldn't be hearing my thoughts right now, could you?"

"I guess not."

"It's a very tasty cake too, but a little crummy for my taste."

"Yes it is, but I forgot the recipe, could you tell me it again?" she asked.

"Of course," said the nice man. "First, you need wheat flour, a pinch of salt, butter, sugar, milk and baking powder." From somewhere music started playing.

"Is that all?" Carrie Lynn asked.

"No, you need an extract of a root found on the island called sasafr…"

She didn't hear what the man said, but she did recognize the song, it was the Beach Boys singing "California Girls" and it seemed to grow louder as the man's voice started to fade. She thought that it was odd to hear them in this place. "I'm sorry, I didn't hear that last part," Carrie Lynn shouted. "That music was too loud…do you like the Beach Boys?"

"Who are the Beach Boys?" the man asked.

"Never mind," she said. "What kind of root was that?"

"It's sassafra…"

Knock, knock, knock.

"Carrie Lynn." Over the Beach Boys song and the man's voice, she heard her father calling.

"Dad?" she said in a groggy voice. "What are you doing here?"

"I'm waking you up, honey."

"Not now, he's telling me what kind of root I need," the girl mumbled.

"Oh no, not another gardener!" Michael said, laughing. "Come on, sweetie, we have to take your project to school. Boy, you sure are a heavy sleeper. Your alarm clock's been on for ten minutes. Don't you hear the music? It's loud enough?"

"What are the Beach Boys doing here?" she said, still in a daze.

"Come on, honey, we have to take your project in to school today remember?"

"Oh yeah," Carrie Lynn said, finally realizing where she was.

Michael turned off the radio.

TWELVE

The parking lot at school was jam packed this morning with students bringing in their projects, and right with them was Carrie Lynn. Dad had put everything in the van before he left for work, and Mom drove her in to help set up. The halls were full of children and parents and teachers all going their separate ways.

Carrie Lynn carried her cakes and Katherine had the display board. As they made their way to the multi-purpose room, they ran into Jenny and Kim Bayer.

"Hello Katherine," Jenny said. "Well, this is almost over with. Aren't you glad? I am because I can finally get this mold out of my house."

"Boy, you did a great job on your display, Kimmie," Carrie Lynn's mom said. Then she read the title of Kim's project. *Fungus Among Us*. "That's cute."

"Thanks," Kim said. "Mom helped a lot, and Dad came up with the title."

"Mom and Dad helped me do my display, but I did the experiment all by myself," Carrie Lynn said proudly.

"She really did," Katherine said. "She wouldn't let anyone help her. And I think she did a really good job."

"Well, we better get in there and see where they want us

to set up," Jenny said. They all proceeded to the designated area and set up their displays. The parents left, the children made their way to their rooms and school started (although a little late) as usual.

That afternoon Katherine heard the school bus outside and met Carrie Lynn at the front door. She asked her how the day went.

"Oh fine," she said.

"Everybody get their projects in ok?"

"Yeah, all except Maurice Simpson. How's your school work so far this week? Are you going to have a good Friday folder?" Mom asked.

"I guess so," she said, a little apprehensively.

"You should, after the way you caught on when Matthew tutored you last weekend."

"Yeah!" Carrie Lynn said with a nervous laugh. She wished her mother would change the subject.

"Well, I guess the judging is going on right now," said Mom.

"Yeah, they were looking at the projects when we were getting on the bus. Are we going over to the school to see the fair?"

"As soon as your father gets home. I'm sure you will get a ribbon, you did such a good job."

I hope I get something, so my geography quiz won't look so bad, Carrie Lynn thought.

"Go on up and change into your play clothes and do your reading, ok?"

"I've finished my book, Mom. All I have to do now is write my report. I was going to do that now, ok?"

"Good girl," her mom said.

Carrie Lynn saw Hazel walk by. She scooped her up, draped her over her shoulder, and dragging her book bag behind her went off to her room. Katherine started dinner. Matthew came home said, "Hi" to his mom and went to his room.

"Don't play your guitar, your sister's doing her homework," Katherine said.

"Aw Mom!"

About 6:00, Dad arrived and was pleasantly surprised to find that dinner was cooking and chicken Parmesan was on the menu.

"Mmm, is there anything I can help you with Kathy?" he said as he kissed his wife.

"No, you just go relax and get ready to go to the science fair," she said.

"Am I in the right house?" he said with a smile.

"Ha, ha," was her reply.

That evening the school parking lot was full, as everyone was anxious to go to the fair. The Fosters started in the library to see the younger grades' projects, and they worked their way up to the fifth grade level where Carrie Lynn's would be.

"Boy," Matthew said. "Some of these are pretty dumb."

"You have to remember," Katherine said. "These are kindergarten and first graders, they'll get better."

Presentation is important to catch the eye of the judges, but the major ingredient of a science project is the actual experimentation. A good idea for a science project can be lost if it is presented wrong or if the experiment is done poorly.

This time Carrie Lynn was right on the mark in both cases. Her display was attractive and well designed and her idea, hypothesis and results were just what the judges were looking for. In a unanimous decision her project was judged best in show!

"Carrie Lynn, look!" her mom said as they saw the ribbon hanging from the display board.

"Congratulations, honey!" Dad said as he gave her a big hug.

"Wow," Carrie Lynn said, thinking there might be some mistake. *I would have been happy with second or third place but best in show, wow! Now maybe my grade on the quiz won't look so bad.*

"I knew all along you'd do good there, pee wee," Matthew said. "'Specially with my help."

"Gee thanks, Matt," she said. Even his sarcasm wasn't going to spoil this moment.

Carrie Lynn basked in the glow of the event, and then they looked around at the other projects. She tried to appreciate them but she just couldn't get over her best in show prize. They ran into Kim's family and Kim ran up to proudly announce that she had taken second place in the fifth grade level.

"Congratulations, Kimmie," Katherine said.

"And congratulations to you, young lady," Jenny said. "Best in show."

"Yeah, how about that?" Michael said. "Well, she did work hard on this one."

"Both of them did," Katherine said. "And they both did

very well."

On the ride home Michael took them by Patterson's for some ice cream to celebrate. This time Matthew was allowed to get whatever he wanted. As the kids ran ahead, Katherine said to Michael, "See...best in show, still don't think our little girl is a genius?" Michael just rolled his eyes.

The next day during the morning announcements all of the winners of the science fair were mentioned. The best in show winner was announced last and when the principal read the name Carrie Lynn Foster, the whole class broke out in applause. Carrie Lynn turned bright red as Mrs. Collison asked her to stand up and take a bow.

The principal reminded them that all of the first place winning projects would go to the state competition and if there was a winner there they could go to the national science fair in Washington, DC.

That Friday when Carrie Lynn brought home her papers for the week, she was very nervous about the C she got on her geography quiz. But, to her surprise her mom barely mentioned it. After all it was the only C paper she got that week. Three A's, two B's and all the rest very goods. She guessed that because of her winning science project Mom was going to let her slide on that one.

Well, Carrie Lynn did take her project to the state competition for the fifth grade where she was asked by three judges to explain her experiment and exactly how she did it. Because she had done it all by herself she knew the exact procedure and was able to answer all of the questions precisely.

She won the state competition.

She then took it to the national science fair and won a respectable fourth place out of the entire country. Her mom and dad were beside themselves with pride for their little girl.

A few weeks later, as Carrie Lynn sat on the porch brushing Hazel, she was telling to her about all the events that happened recently.

"Well Hazey, I tried my other cakes but they didn't work. They didn't taste the same, they didn't crumble, and they didn't give me super powers. I guess the right recipe was just in that one. Anyway, I did learn that if you do the work and know the answers then you don't have to cheat to pass the tests. But, it sure was fun! Remember when Matthew hit himself in the face with that ice cream cone?" she said laughing. "And when he shot across the yard with the wheel barrow? I'd like to have the special cake just so I could do things like that to him all the time!" she laughed again. "Do you know that every now and then all of a sudden I'll hear someone's thoughts or move something, but it's not like it was before. Oh well, the book said it's been 10,000 years since they first made the cakes, I guess it'll be another 10,000 before we see them again. Huh, Hazie?"

Then Hazel looked up and Carrie Lynn heard a little voice think, "Maybe not!"

THE END

Printed in the United States
19600LVS00006B/355-360